Basket Weaver
and
Catches Many Mice

by Janet Gill · illustrated by Yangsook Choi

ALFRED A. KNOPF 🐎 NEW YORK

For Jane Yolen,
who showed me the wonder of words
—J.G.

For my brothers
Junho and Seungdo
—Y.C.

Library of Congress Cataloging-in-Publication Data
Gill, Janet.
Basket Weaver and Catches Many Mice / by Janet Gill ; illustrated by Yangsook Choi.
p. cm.
Summary: A little gray cat saves the day when Basket Weaver is ordered into a competition
to make the perfect basket for the emperor's newborn daughter.
[1. Basket making—Fiction. 2. Cats—Fiction.] I. Choi, Yangsook, ill. II. Title.
PZ7.G39865Bas   1999
[E]—dc21   98-26859
ISBN 0-679-88922-1 (trade)
ISBN 0-679-98922-6 (lib. bdg.)

Printed in Hong Kong
10 9 8 7 6 5 4 3 2 1

First Edition

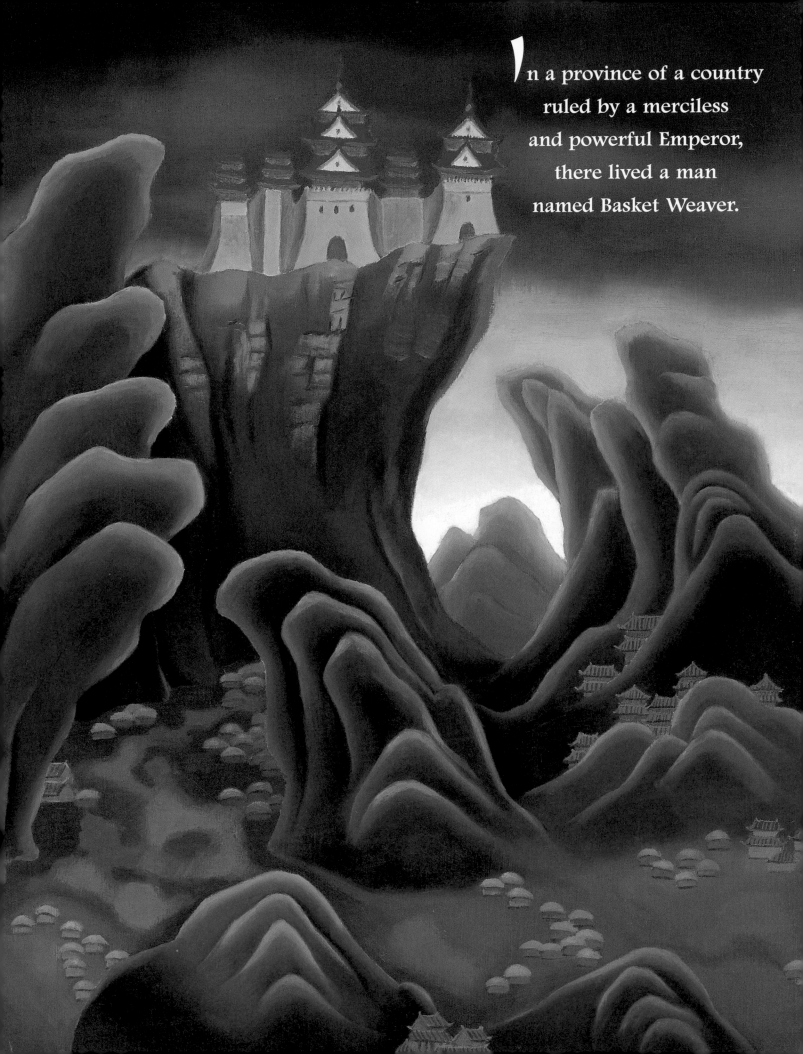

In a province of a country
ruled by a merciless
and powerful Emperor,
there lived a man
named Basket Weaver.

All day, every day, Basket Weaver worked at his trade. He made baskets for housewives to store food and to steam fish and vegetables, others for workers to carry supplies. But the most important baskets were the ones he made for the newborn babies. These were the beds they would sleep in their first year, and into each he wove the spirit of the child.

When he made a bed for an infant named Stone Cutter, Basket Weaver used rushes from the marsh behind his house. Rushes bend but do not break when the wind blows strong. He added scarlet, gold, and blue feathers from birds that flitted through the marsh, so Stone Cutter's heart would be light, though the stones he worked were heavy.

For a tiny girl named Cares for Books, who would someday watch over the province's treasured volumes, Basket Weaver wove the ferns that love cool, quiet spots. He added grass roots, for as those roots fan below ground, so would Cares for Books spread knowledge. Finally, he tucked in owl feathers, for wisdom.

Basket Weaver's home stood on the bank of a stream. One spring day, he scooped a drowning cat from the rushing waters. After drying the cat's gray-striped fur, he gave her a bowl of warm milk, then placed her in a basket on the hearth. She curled up and went to sleep.

Basket Weaver felt pleased she had chosen to stay with him. In his country, cats received much honor. Everyone knew that cats followed their own minds and always made wise choices.

Now, this cat was not so young that she still needed her mother, but young enough that in the moonlight she stalked and pounced on shadows. Basket Weaver called her Catches Many Mice, for he believed everyone should have a name to live up to.

On summer mornings, Basket Weaver sat on his porch with Catches Many Mice, listening to the rippling stream, the rustling rushes, the twittering birds, and felt content.

One day after the trees had thrown their leaves to the fall wind, a man appeared at Basket Weaver's door. His name was Delivers Messages, and he came from the Emperor.

Basket Weaver worried as he set out refreshments. What could the great Emperor want of him?

"Last week," Delivers Messages began, "the Empress gave birth to her first child, a girl. In time, this baby will be our Empress. The Emperor orders the basket weavers of each of the four provinces to weave a bed for her. He and the Empress will choose the best one. Its weaver will live in the palace as Basket Weaver to the Emperor and will be granted three requests."

"A fine reward," Basket Weaver said.

"However," Delivers Messages added, "those weavers whose beds do not please the Emperor will be sent to work in the mines for seven years."

The mines! Underground day after day. Basket Weaver struggled to keep his face from showing his dismay.

"You and the bed must appear at the palace in seven days," Delivers Messages said, and left.

"I would hate leaving my home to live in the palace," Basket Weaver told Catches Many Mice, "but going into the mines would be like dying a little every day." He sighed. Running away would do no good. The Emperor's soldiers would find him, and then the punishment would be ten times worse.

That evening, the wind howled around Basket Weaver's house. He sat close by the fire. "What kind of person must an Empress be?" he mused.

From her basket, Catches Many Mice watched him with wise eyes.

"I shall weave the bed from the ivy climbing the stream's bank," he said at last. "Ivy's touch is soft, but its hold is tight. Through the vines I'll entwine cherry branches. The tree bears wonderful fruit, and its beauty grows richer with age. Pink-everlasting flowers will promise her long life. And for happiness, the marsh birds' bright feathers." Basket Weaver gazed at Catches Many Mice. "That is the best I can do."

The next morning, Basket Weaver collected the ivy. Then he and Catches Many Mice traveled to the hills beyond the village for pink-everlasting. The wind had buffeted the flowers, and he chose the least tattered blossoms. He gathered cherry branches in an orchard on the way home. Moving everything into his workroom, he began to weave.

Five days he worked, stopping only to eat and sleep. When the bed was almost finished, Basket Weaver studied it.

The finest bed I've ever woven, he thought. *Feathers will make it perfect.*

But to his horror, he found but one scarlet feather in the cupboard. One feather meant the baby would smile but seldom laugh. And he'd find no more feathers in the marsh. The birds had flown away for the winter. His shoulders drooped. His hopes of being chosen faded.

The following morning, the Emperor's men arrived to carry the bed to the palace. Basket Weaver would follow on horseback the next day.

After they left, he gazed around. For seven years he would not see the bright birds, not hear the rippling stream. Sorrowing, he turned from the scene, then frowned. Catches Many Mice was not in her basket. And though he called her all day, she did not appear.

She's made the wise choice to run away, he thought as he prepared for his trip. But the idea of her leaving him struck pain in his heart.

When Basket Weaver departed the next morning, snowflakes were flurrying down. He rode huddled beneath a blanket and arrived at the palace at dusk. Even the wonder of that magnificent structure could not push away his fear. Tomorrow he'd meet the Emperor.

The next morning, dressed in his finest robe, he presented himself at the throne room. The three other basket weavers were waiting, all looking as frightened as he felt. When the great doors opened, the four marched in and knelt in a line across the middle of the room.

The Emperor and the Empress entered, and Basket Weaver remained bowed with the others until the two were seated on their thrones. Looking up, he gazed directly at the Emperor.

Not someone to make angry, Basket Weaver judged.

The Emperor clapped his hands. Servants lined the four beds up before the throne, Basket Weaver's at the end. The first two had many bright feathers. All had pink-everlasting. Over the sides of the one next to his, Basket Weaver saw a lining of owl feathers.

He'd forgotten wisdom! He held back a groan.

The Emperor and Empress moved to the first bed. It was woven of birch branches, a tree that bends in the wind but does not break.

But once bent, Basket Weaver thought, *it never stands straight again.*

They moved on. Cherry branches shaped the next.

He's given her beauty and strength. Cherry trees stand firm in a strong wind.

Rushes formed the third. The Empress smiled when she gazed at the feather lining. Beside Basket Weaver, the maker of that bed sighed softly.

He's won, Basket Weaver thought. The sorrow of loss filled him. Not wishing to see the Emperor and Empress pass his bed without a glance, he stared down at his robe.

Hearing a gasp, he looked up. The Empress was reaching into his basket. From it, she lifted a kitten. Then out leaped a gray-striped cat.

Catches Many Mice! His cat and her kitten in the bed of a future Empress. He would surely lose his head for this.

The Emperor approached the weavers.

"Whose cats are these?" he demanded.

"Mine, Sire." Basket Weaver could scarcely answer for the thumping of his heart.

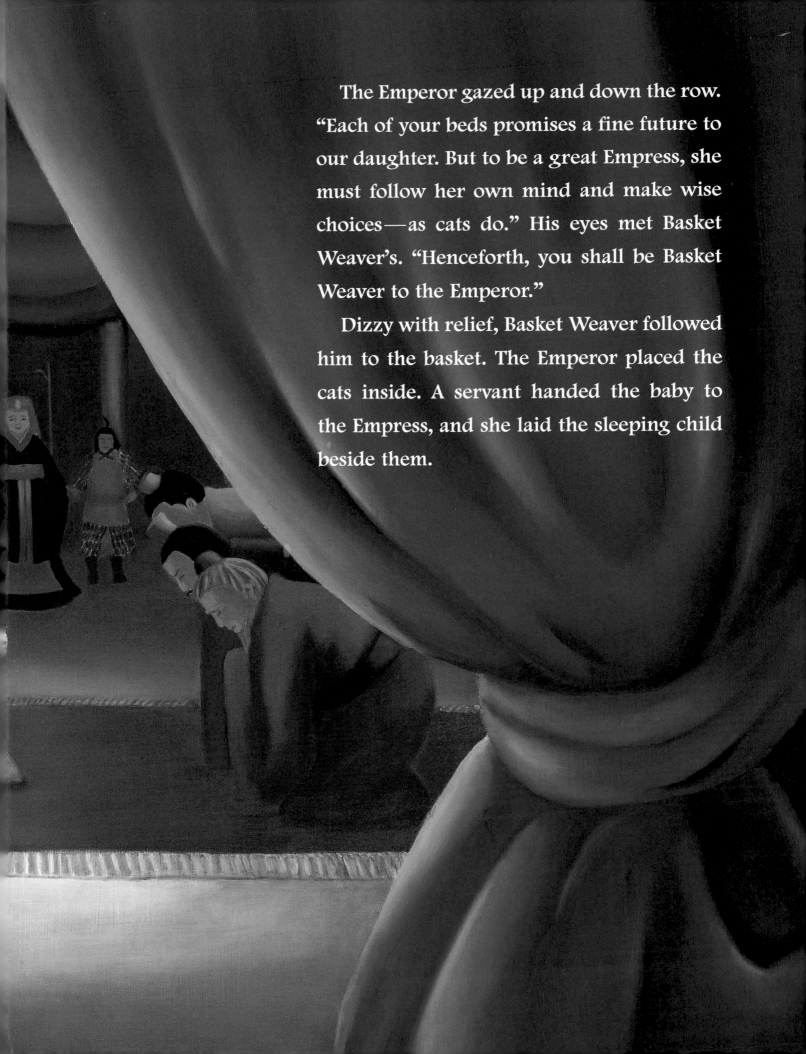

The Emperor gazed up and down the row. "Each of your beds promises a fine future to our daughter. But to be a great Empress, she must follow her own mind and make wise choices—as cats do." His eyes met Basket Weaver's. "Henceforth, you shall be Basket Weaver to the Emperor."

Dizzy with relief, Basket Weaver followed him to the basket. The Emperor placed the cats inside. A servant handed the baby to the Empress, and she laid the sleeping child beside them.

"Have you considered your three requests?" the Emperor asked. "Gold, perhaps? Fine furs? Precious gems?"

Basket Weaver bowed low. "I will be proud to be your weaver," he said, "but I request I be allowed to return to my home. I can make all the baskets you need there."

The Emperor scowled.

"Next," Basket Weaver hurried on, "when the kitten is old enough to leave its mother, I would like to take my cat home with me."

The Emperor's lip jutted out over his beard.

Basket Weaver gazed at his fellow weavers. Misery showed in their faces. "Last, I request that these men be spared the mines. As you said, Sire, they did their best for our future Empress. Why should they be punished?"

The Emperor's chest swelled. His face reddened. "How dare you question my decision?" he boomed, and stepped toward the third basket.

Oh, no, Basket Weaver thought. *I asked too much. How could I have been so foolish?*

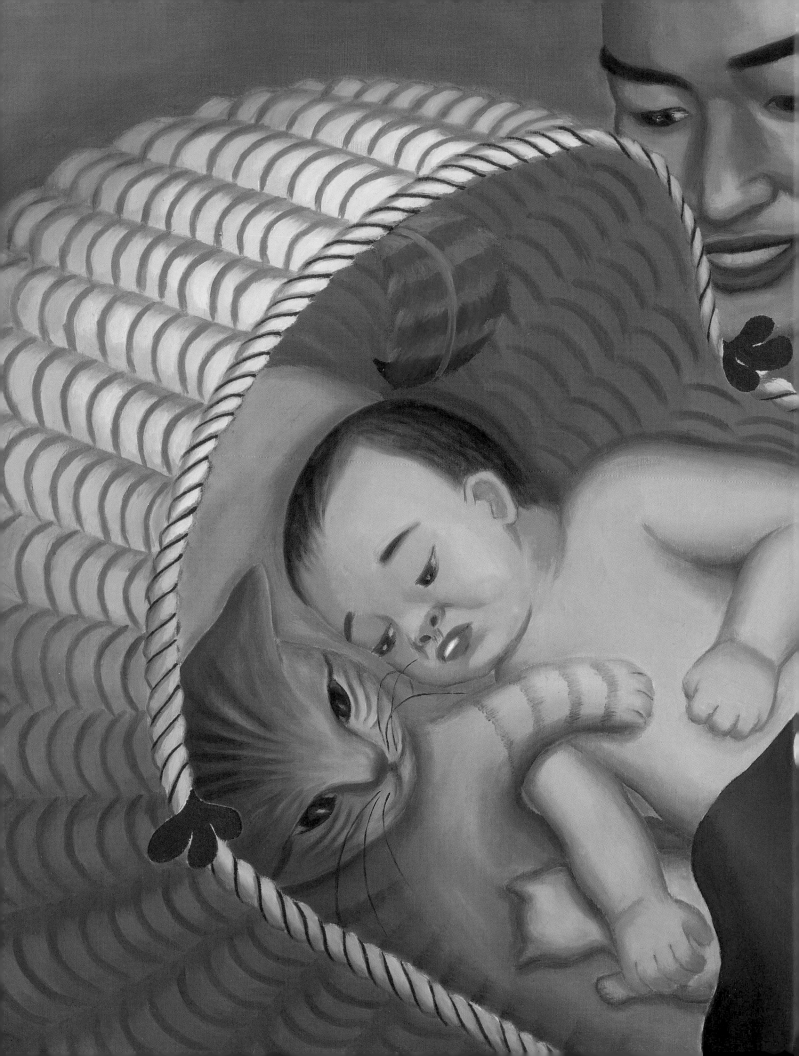

Just then the baby whimpered. As the three looked down, she placed a tiny hand on the kitten.

"Look, my Esteemed Husband," the Empress said, "our daughter has made her first wise choice."

And thus, when leaf buds on the trees swelled to bursting, Basket Weaver and Catches Many Mice returned home. He hired villagers to help make the many baskets the Emperor ordered. And on summer mornings, Basket Weaver sat on his porch with Catches Many Mice, listening to the rippling stream, the rustling rushes, the twittering birds, and felt content.